For Benjamin with love

Swankypants
Books

Published by Swankypants Books

Printed in China

The magical world of Swankypants

A little owl called Hooty

Early one evening high up in a tree,
Hooty the owl came out for his tea.

He sat on a branch and looked out at the sky,
and waited for insects fluttering by.

Swankypants watched from the garden below,
Hooty couldn't catch things, for he was too slow.

"Come on Hooty, fly down from the tree,
come down here with Chatterbox and me."

"I'm too scared, the tree is too high,
there's plenty of insects up here in the sky!"

So the two cats watched by the light of the moon,
wondering if Hooty might catch something soon.

Chatterbox asked, *"Why won't Hooty fly,
lets ask the barn owl, perhaps he'll know why?"*

So the cats found the barn owl sat in the tree,
told him of Hooty, whom they went to see.

And there at the top of the very tall tree,
sat little Hooty still waiting for tea.

The wise old owl flew to the scared little bird,
"come follow me friend, not to fly is absurd!"

All at once little Hooty started to fly,
and followed the barn owl swooping the sky.

So now every night, they fly through the trees,
flying high on the warm summer breeze.

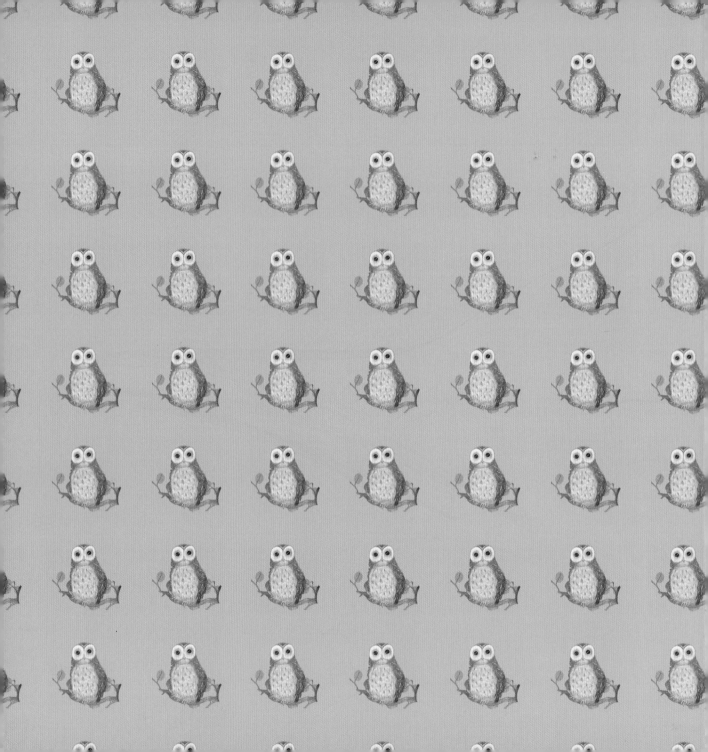